Svenja Herrmann was born in Frankfurt on the Main, Germany; she grew up in the canton of Zug, Switzerland. Herrmann studied German literature, legal history, and constitutional law and today works as a writer. For many years she has worked in education, where she has been inspiring children and adolescents through literature. She lives in Zurich, Switzerland.

Józef Wilkoń was born in Bogucice near Krakow (Poland). He studied painting and art history in Krakow. He is one of the best-known illustrators for children and adults in Poland. Józef Wilkoń is inspired by a variety of sources, such as the folk art of his homeland and ancient Greek paintings. He lives with his son near Warsaw.

Copyright © 2020 by NordSüd Verlag AG, CH-8050 Zürich, Switzerland.
First published in Switzerland under the title *Wolfskinder*.
English text copyright © 2020 by NorthSouth Books, Inc., New York 10016.
Translated by David Henry Wilson.
All rights reserved.

First published in the United States, Great Britain, Canada, Australia, and New Zealand in 2020 by NorthSouth Books, Inc., an imprint of NordSüd Verlag AG, CH-8050 Zürich, Switzerland.
Distributed in the United States by NorthSouth Books, Inc., New York 10016.
Library of Congress Cataloging-in-Publication Data is available.

ISBN: 978-0-7358-4397-4

1 3 5 7 9 · 10 8 6 4 2

Printed at Livonia Print, Riga, Latvia, 2019
www.northsouth.com

Svenja Herrmann   Józef Wilkoń

The Little Wolves

Translated by David Henry Wilson

North
South

One starlit night, a little wolf woke up in her cave. Her mother was out hunting and so she risked taking a few steps toward the entrance. The sweet spring air stung her nose, and she let out a soft whimper.

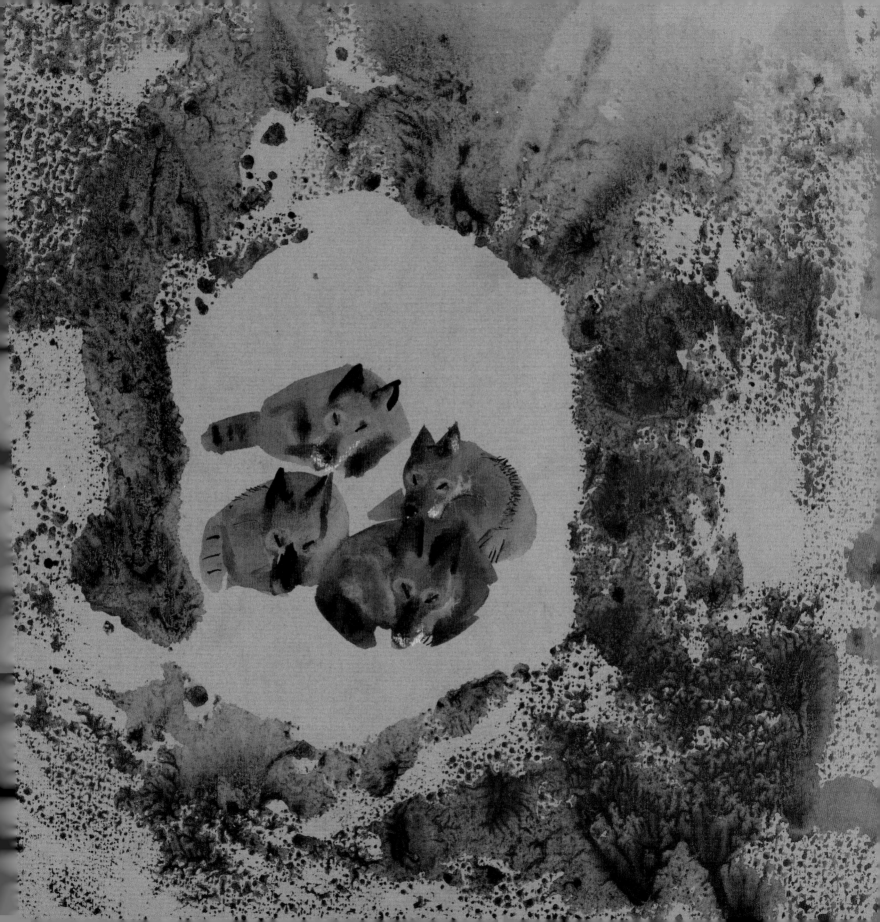

Her sister and two brothers woke up as well and came to sniff the forest-scented darkness. Now the little wolf felt brave enough to go all the way to the entrance. The others followed her toward the very special scent of the forest, which had never smelled so strong and so irresistible before.

One more step and then another, and finally they were out of the cave in a tight little line.

The pine trees towered high above them, seeming almost to reach up to the stars. It was a mysterious night, and the eyes of the four cubs shone in the dark. Or was it the stars reflected in their eyes?

The sparkling roof of heaven seemed both near and far, and the trees seemed endlessly tall; and yet all of them at the same time bent over the little wolf pack as if to protect them.

The young wolves wandered through the forest for a long time until the sun began to drive the darkness away. It was now the sun's turn to take over, and its rays warmed the skin of the cubs. After their long walk, the light sparked courage and a desire for adventure in their spirits.

They came to a clearing and a little lake. Some old and very leafy lime trees stood on the shore like sentinels in the sunlight. Cautiously the cubs approached the water and lined up beside it, ready for anything.

They looked at the mirrorlike surface and saw four little wolves, just like themselves, looking back at them. The shock made them all retreat, but they soon ventured back to the water's edge. Then their fur stood on end.

Once again, the four little wolves saw the strange water wolves looking curiously back at them. What should they do? Jump in and make friends, one, two, three, four? Still they did nothing.

The little leader finally plucked up her courage and was the first to jump into the water.

One, two . . . It took a little longer before cubs three and four followed. All the hearts were beating fast.

Their paws burrowed through the cool water. It was quite different from walking on the soft floor of the forest. The water slid away from under them, and they felt featherlight. Drops swirled around their heads and tickled their noses.

But what was strange was the fact that none of the four water wolves were anywhere to be seen. The four little wolves had not turned into eight after all.

And so one, two, three, four wolf cubs climbed out of the water and clambered up to the shore of the lake. They shook their wet fur, spraying drops of water in all directions.

Their tummies were rumbling after all
the swimming and the excitement. But now,
standing directly in front of them was a
small, prickly ball, which slowly raised its
head and looked at them curiously.

Two of the little wolves greedily pounced on it and quickly found that it was not for eating! The fine spikes gave them both painful stings. The hedgehog then hurried away, leaving the hungry cubs behind.

Once more the four of them set off, going deeper and deeper into the forest. The day was now drawing to a close, and darkness fell. Very soon the moon began to shine again through the tall pine trees. It spread its silver light over the soft forest floor, but it was not bright enough to lighten the darkness, which became scarier and scarier with every step they took. They moved slowly and cautiously, close together in a line.

The trunks of the pines grew ever darker, and the stars seemed farther away than they had been the night before. They missed their mother, and their hunger was beginning to hurt.

Nevertheless, they bravely made their way onward through the darkness. But this time they kept stopping, looking to the left and right, right and left, over and over again.

Who might be hiding behind the tree trunks? All the smells were unfamiliar, and there was no sign of their mother. Far and wide, nothing! How much farther could they go?

For the first time, four howls echoed through the silent forest. These were not the high squeals of little cubs. These were wolf howls!

The cubs went on until they reached the edge of the forest. Then suddenly they heard a magical sound they had never heard before. It was a continuous cry quite different from that of their mother but also soothing. *Huhuuuu, huhuuuu!*

The four cubs could not take their eyes off this extraordinary creature. They completely forgot their hunger and their homesickness. But then the owl spread his wings and silently flew out of the forest. The four cubs watched him go, still entranced by the sight of him and the sound of his strange cry. After a while, they made their way onward, heads bowed. The silver moon was still illuminating the night.

Oh! What is a hunter doing in our story?
Is he asleep? Is he stirring? Look out, little wolves!

The hunter woke up, but the four cubs were too quick for him, and in a flash they disappeared into the shelter of the dark forest. And so, luckily, our story can continue.

Behind every tree trunk the cubs hoped
to find the way back to their cave. They were
very hungry and very tired. The little leader
began to utter quiet howls, and the others
joined in. That had helped them before,
and it helped them again. They must stay
together and not give up hope. They listened
carefully in case their mother answered.
Nothing.

They howled and listened, over and over
again. But the forest remained silent.

Then, at long last, from far away they heard a howl that warmed their hearts and magically drew them in that direction. At once they answered the call and began to run through the dense forest, past the old lime trees, and away from the four water wolves in the pond.

The owl glided above them, and the moon threw its silver beams into the forest. Suddenly everything was simple again, and the little leader knew exactly where she was going.

Once more they heard the howl of their mother, who had just returned from the hunt. Now she was very near.

The cubs found the opening to their cave and crawled inside. The little leader at once jumped up to embrace her mother. But her mother growled. She had been worried sick about her cubs and was not in a mood to play with them or feed them.

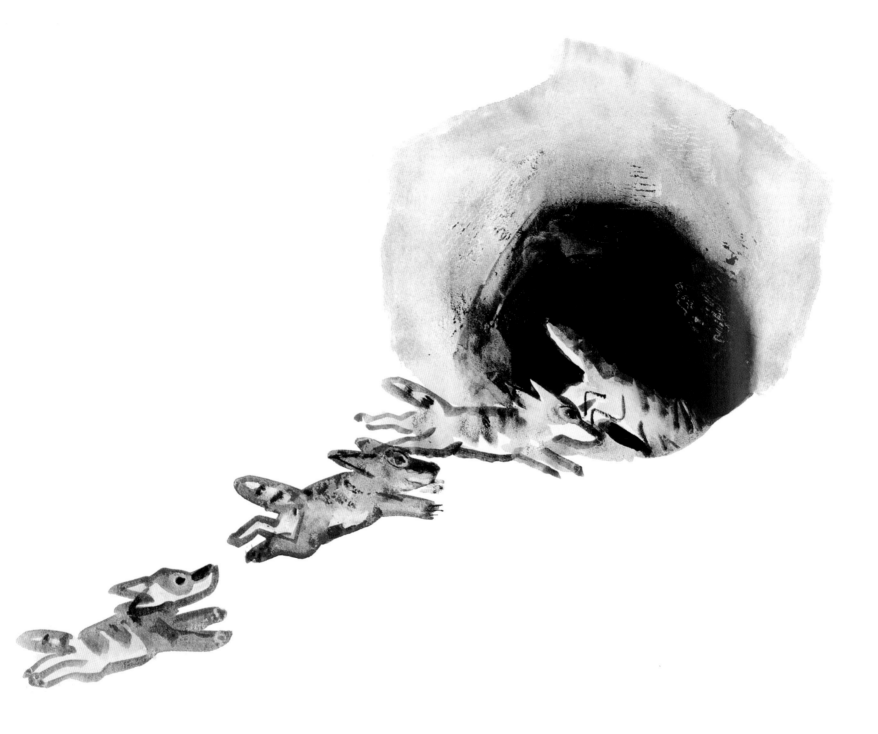

Then the four little wolves lowered their heads and put their tails between their legs. But this did not last long, and soon all was forgiven. They snuggled up close to one another and rested. They had had their first adventure as a pack, and there would be many more to follow.